STAY COLORFUL!

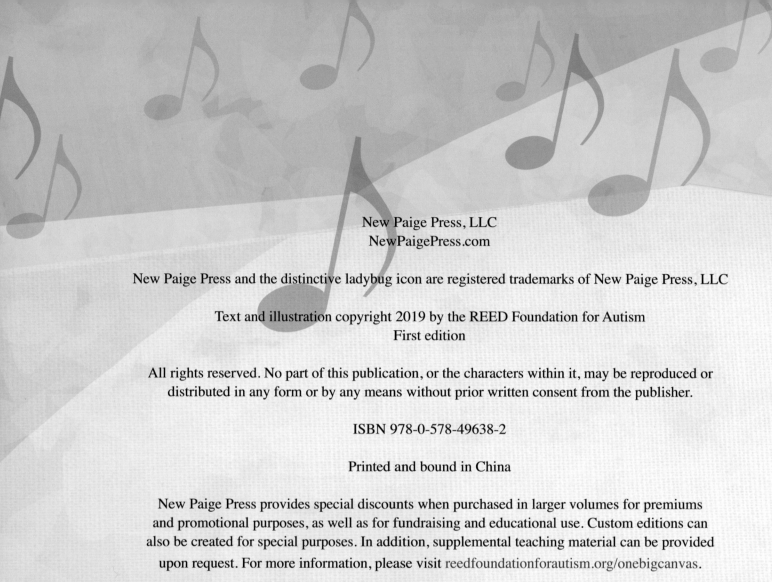

New Paige Press, LLC
NewPaigePress.com

Text and illustration copyright 2019 by the REED Foundation for Autism
First edition

ISBN 978-0-578-49638-2

Printed and bound in China

New Paige Press provides special discounts when purchased in larger volumes for premiums
and promotional purposes, as well as for fundraising and educational use. Custom editions can
also be created for special purposes. In addition, supplemental teaching material can be provided
upon request. For more information, please visit reedfoundationforautism.org/onebigcanvas.

The Masterpiece

Written by
Jay Miletsky

Painted by
Luis Peres

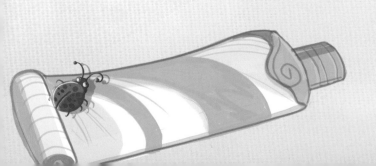

In the back of the studio,
behind lumps of clay,
to the left of a canvas
where the paint cans would spray,
on a dusty old table
that was littered with chalk,
the paintbrushes gathered
for an artistic talk.

The first one to speak
was a paintbrush named Reese,
who said, "Let's create...
a grand masterpiece!
Something with color,
to fill many pages,
to be remembered by all,
and to last through the ages."

The paintbrushes cheered, and raced to begin,
except for one brush, who didn't join in.
A brush named Estelle sat off to the side
and stared at the wall, with her eyes opened wide.
She rocked back and forth, as though in a small boat,
and sang to herself with a single, low note.

Her single-note song, her continuous hum,
and the others knew well where this hum had come from.
They had heard it before and knew this was her way,
then two went on over to ask her to play.
They gave her some paint -
red, yellow, and blue -
"If you'd like to come paint,
we'd love to have you."

So the brushes got started,
with large, vibrant strokes,
painting valleys and lakes,
elm trees and oaks.
They created a forest
with a sleepy, brown fox
and, on one of the hillsides,
they painted some rocks.

They all worked together,
setting mood, theme, and tone,
when they noticed that Byron
had gone off on his own.
He ignored all the others,
he had not made a sound –
he just painted in circles,
around and around.

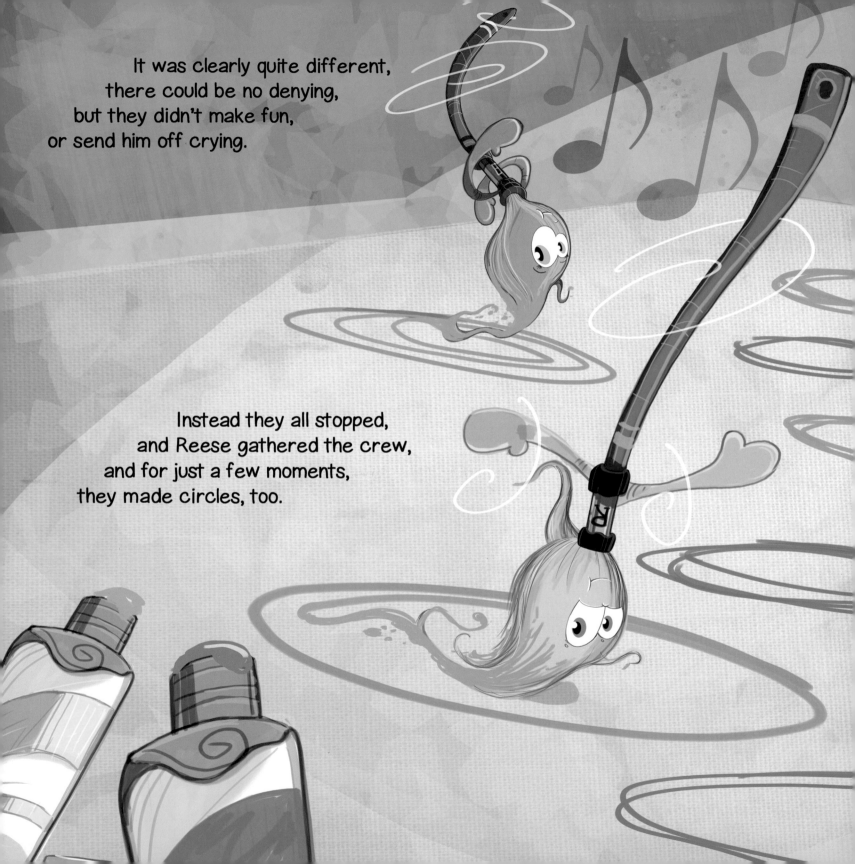

It was clearly quite different,
there could be no denying,
but they didn't make fun,
or send him off crying.

Instead they all stopped,
and Reese gathered the crew,
and for just a few moments,
they made circles, too.

They painted some more and worked well as a team,
when they suddenly heard a

STARTLING
SCREAM!

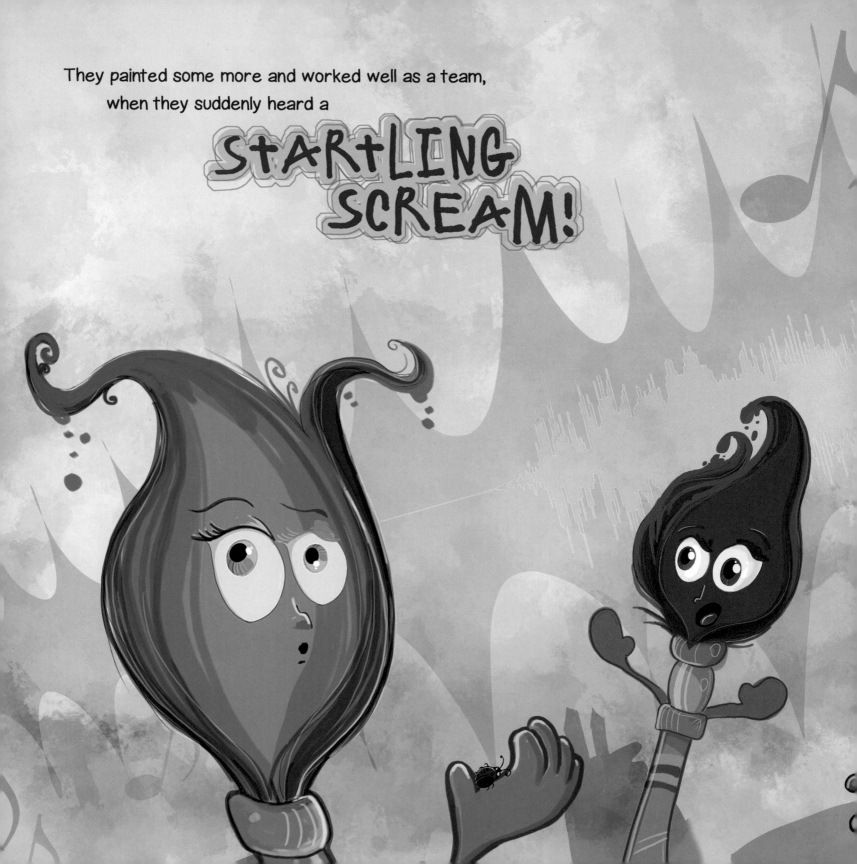

They jumped back in shock and turned 'round to see
that the one who had screamed was a paintbrush named Lee,
who spun all around, shaking all of his bristles,
as paint hit the canvas like green, dotted missiles.
Then he made a green splotch
and an angry green line
while Reese calmed the others:
"Don't worry - it's fine."

"He just can't control it, there's no need to be scared, and the next time it happens, you'll be more prepared."

The outburst had ended, and they all settled down
and added more colors - pink, purple, and brown.

They worked through the day, then stopped and admired
the wisdom their now-painted canvas inspired:
their painting was perfect! It all meshed just fine,
with its colorful circles and angry green line.
It was a true masterpiece – not one thing was wrong...
including the hum of their single-note song.

Meet the Cast of 'The Masterpiece'

CLINICAL ADVISORS

Kelli Fowler, MA, BCBA

Kelli Fowler is a Board Certified Behavior Analyst (BCBA) who holds a Master of Arts in special education and is a certified general and special education teacher. She has been educating children on the autism spectrum since 2004. As the clinical director at REED Academy, Kelli focuses on educational services, behavior, and transition supports. She also works with school districts and other organizations to bring awareness to autism and integrate education into the community.

Joseph Novak, EdD, BCBA-D, CCC-SLP, ATP

Joe Novak is a Board Certified Behavior Analyst-Doctoral Level (BCBA-D) who holds a Doctorate of Education in special education and is an ASHA-certified speech and language pathologist. He is also an adjunct professor at Kean University. As the director of curriculum & technology at REED Academy, Joe oversees speech and language, augmentative communication, curriculum development, and technology initiatives.

BOOK DEVELOPERS

Jay Miletsky, Author

Jay Miletsky is a reformed business author who has turned his attention to the far more creative, exciting, and competitive world of children's picture books. His titles include *Ricky, the Rock that Couldn't Roll*, *The Bear and the Fern*, *Patrick Picklebottom and the Penny Book*, and others.

He credits his daughter, Bria, for inspiring many of his story ideas, and his fiancé, Amanda, for pointing out how to make each book a whole lot better. He can be reached at www.JayMiletsky.com.

Luis Peres, Artist/Illustrator

Born in the south of Portugal, Luis has been illustrating professionaly since 1992. His work includes children's books, book covers, short stories, postcards, and board games. He also illustrates regularly for publishing companies specializing in school books. Luis is happiest when illustrating imaginary worlds, whimsical characters, or anything related to fantasy and sci-fi landscapes.

Luis' work can be viewed at www.icreateworlds.com.

REED FOUNDATION FOR AUTISM

An initiative of the REED Foundation for Autism, the "One Big Canvas" series seeks to celebrate differences, showcasing how each individual, regardless of his or her own unique qualities, can be an integral part of a much larger picture. Autism is a highly prevalent and often misunderstood neurological disability. Our hope is that these positive and engaging children's stories will promote acceptance, understanding, and kindness for all. To learn more about Autism Spectrum Disorder, please visit reedfoundationforautism.org.

The "One Big Canvas" series is funded in part through a grant from the Special Child Health and Autism Registry, New Jersey Department of Health.

REED Foundation for Autism is a 50 l(c)(3)